# INTRODUCTION

## by Child Brain Injury Trust

Every 30 minutes, a child or young person will acquire a brain injury. This could be the result of an accident, fall, an illness such as meningitis or encephalitis, a poisoning, a stroke or a brain tumour.

A brain injury has a devastating and life-long impact on the child and their whole family. Bones can mend and scars can heal but a brain injury stays with you for life and impacts on everything you think, feel and do.

The Child Brain Injury Trust is the only charity in the UK that supports the whole family - children, young people, their parents and carers as well as professionals following brain injury. The charity provides support and information and helps families come to terms with what has happened and how to deal with the uncertainty that the future may hold.

## A Message from Beverley Turner, Ambassador of the Child Brain Injury Trust

Beverley Turner, Ambassador of the Child Brain Injury Trust, is an accomplished journalist, author of Touching Distance and TV and radio presenter. She is a mother of three and is married to Olympic rower James Cracknell OBE.

Acquired brain injuries affect thousands of families each year, but the impact is never greater than when it occurs to a child. Greater understanding of the problems which arise is crucial in helping more families to stay together after such a life-changing event and yet it can be hard to find advice, support and guidance when tragedy strikes. That's why I'm happy to lend my support to the Child Brain Injury Trust and in particular to the resources and information it provides to families and to professionals. I am sure these books will also help parents and teachers and anyone else who has been affected by acquired brain injury to feel that they are not alone.

# 1.WAKING UP

James opened his eyes and saw his mum with her good morning smile, gently tugging his arm. She was saying that he should get up. For a moment he was cross – he had been in such a warm, comfy sleep – but then he was excited.

He loved going to school and remembered that today was going to be even better because they would be baking special cakes. He loved cakes, too, and Mrs Jones had said that he could bring some home for Mum, Dad and Megan, his little sister.

James was thinking about cakes when his mum called him again to hurry up. He was sure he had only been thinking about them for a moment but he hadn't started to get dressed yet.

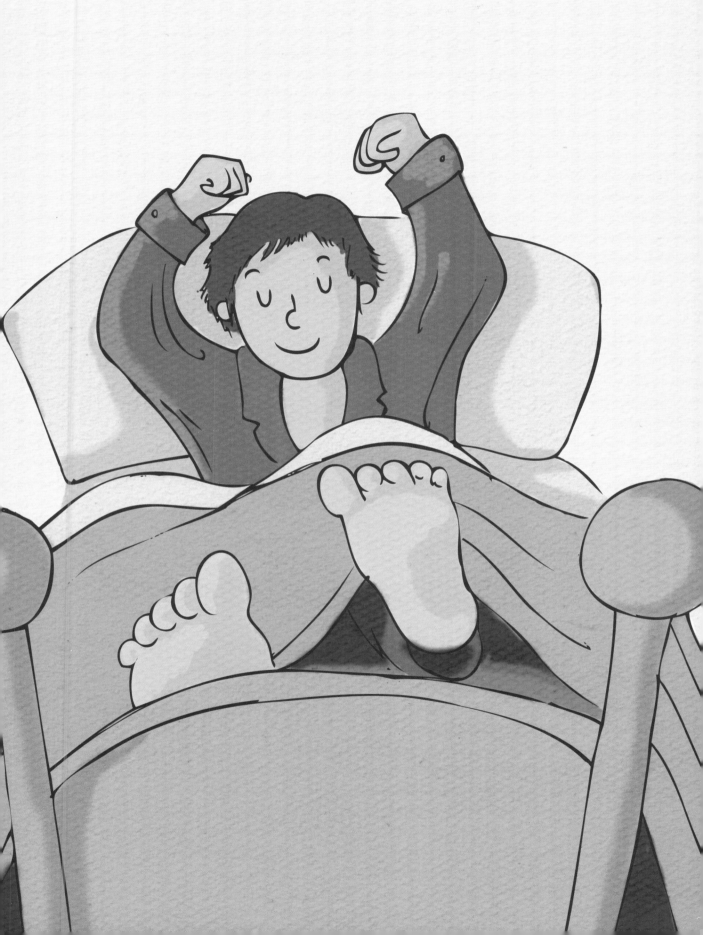

James picked up his socks and shoes. Brown socks. Brown, like chocolate. Was it chocolate cakes they were going to make? Had he got chocolate to take to school? Perhaps he forgot. He looked for it.

His mum called again. She said he had been ages and he must come now so he could have breakfast before school. But he had only just got up! Where did he put his shoes? He was searching for something wasn't he? Mum came to his room and she was cross because he hadn't started getting dressed. She started to pick up his clothes and tried to help him put them on. He hated it when she moved them about.

This was not the way he got dressed and he was thinking about something exciting but now he had forgotten! Mum was complaining because his shoes weren't where

they should be. She told him to start his breakfast but he never starts breakfast without his shoes. James could hear his mum complaining and Megan was crying. He couldn't find things and couldn't remember the good thing that he was thinking about. His head began to hurt.

Mum shouted that he must come for breakfast straight away. James shouted back and something in his head seemed to be telling him to throw his favourite robot toy against the wall. The noises in the house seemed louder, he yelled and the whole room went very dark.

James realised that he was under his bed. It was very quiet. He crawled out and his favourite toy was in pieces on the floor. There were ripped pages from his best story book on the bed. His clothes

were spread all over the room. Did he do this? How could he make everything go back to normal?

Suddenly James saw Buddy, his best friend. Buddy came to visit when James needed him and this time he sat quietly in the corner, watching James with his big brown eyes. Then he came over, licked James' hand and turned towards the cupboard door. James stroked Buddy's soft ears and followed him.

James saw his colour chart with green next to the number 1 at the bottom, going up through yellow, orange and blue to 10 and red at the top. Oh, dear, he had been in that red mood. He was still orange and needed to keep going back towards green to feel happy again and to get things back to normal. He sat down and when he stroked Buddy again, he remembered the

# How do you think James is feeling right now?

cakes and the good day to come. Yellow. He started to pick up the broken and ripped things. His mum came to help and smiled at him. It felt good that everything was going to be right again. He was back at green.

James turned to thank Buddy who barked quickly and looked towards James' other chart on the whiteboard on the wall before he disappeared. Of course! Tomorrow he must remember to look at the picture list on there and cross off things to do when he got up and then he wouldn't be late. It also showed what was happening today so he could remember. The picture list was next to his big egg timer. James liked to show Buddy that he could beat the timer when he was getting dressed!

# 2.SCHOOL

Mum reminded James about the cakes and they checked together that he had everything he needed. He was excited again when he got to school but then when he got to his classroom Mrs Jones, his teacher, wasn't there. There was a different teacher who he didn't know and who told them that Mrs Jones wasn't very well. Miss Johnson and Mr Matthews who helped in the class were there but the new teacher, whose name he couldn't remember, started the day differently. She put them in groups and made him sit opposite Kyle. James was cross because Kyle always looked at him funnily and hit him once last term. He was looking at James again. James kept looking back and didn't hear what that new teacher had told him to do. She said he must listen. How could he listen when Kyle was talking about him now? He glanced at the work that he had been given. He'd never seen this before. It was different and he was scared.

# How do you think James is feeling right now?

He couldn't understand it and didn't know how to do it! He needed his old work back and wanted Miss Johnson or Mr Matthews to get it for him but they were helping other children. He shouted to them but the new teacher said he had to wait and to try the work on his own because he could do it. He couldn't do it because it looked different and Kyle's voice seemed to be getting louder and louder and filling his head! James shouted at Kyle, threw his work on the floor and ran towards the classroom door. Just as he had almost reached it, he looked up and there, in the doorway, was Buddy. James stopped and looked at his kind face. James was so pleased to see him and all the classroom noise seemed to disappear.

Buddy had James' colour chart. He'd got to orange again but just seeing and touching Buddy made him feel more yellow already. Buddy was looking behind James into the classroom and, when he turned round, James saw

# How do you think James is feeling right now?

that Miss Johnson had come over to help him and she'd moved Kyle to another group. James went back to his place. He liked Miss Johnson. He knew her. She explained again what work James had to do and it was the same as he had done before, even though it had looked different. James relaxed and was happy that he knew what to do and he was back at green. He looked over to thank Buddy and he had disappeared but James knew that he was always close by. Then Miss Johnson reminded him about the picture list that he had at school as well so he could see what he had to do and she put it on the table next to him. That was familiar and he felt safe. He remembered that he had a 'time out' card that he could show as well if his head was drumming and he needed to go to the quiet area just outside the classroom. He must use that another time if he was going towards orange on the chart. James finished his work and was proud to get a special sticker from the new teacher. She wasn't so bad after all!

# How do you think James is feeling right now?

Soon it was lunch time which was one of James' favourite times. The dinners at school were very good and today he'd have cake later, which was even better! Then after lunch the new teacher said that as Mrs Jones wasn't there, they would wait and make cakes the next day when she was back. That couldn't happen! They were making cakes today! James didn't understand why this had to be changed and he was angry. He asked Miss Johnson why things had changed. She started to tell him but all James heard was 'not today'. He asked Mr Matthews but he kept talking and James couldn't hear what he said, apart from 'no cakes today'. James asked them again and again and asked the new teacher, too. It wasn't fair, this wasn't what should be happening and he didn't hear what they were saying. In the end the new teacher raised her voice and he heard her say clearly, "James I have told you to stop and listen now to what we are doing next!" She began to read the start of a story. Chocolate cake. Chocolate cake. James

# How do you think James is feeling right now?

couldn't listen and he needed to move about. He stood up, turning away from the teacher and there was Buddy again. Buddy looked towards James' pocket where he kept the 'time out' card. Of course! James couldn't speak but he showed the card to Mr Matthews and he said James could go to the quiet area. Buddy went with him and James sat on the beanbag with his arms around the soft fur on Buddy's neck. He told Buddy why he was cross and Buddy just listened without saying he was wrong. Buddy was never cross and he was always very patient. James began to feel better and the colours were changing. Then Miss Johnson came to see him and told him how great he'd been to use the card and leave rather than getting more cross in the classroom. She gave him some cold juice with a straw and he felt better and better as he gently sucked the drink. Miss Johnson showed him the picture list so he knew what was happening for the rest of the afternoon and said that making cakes would be on tomorrow's list. Buddy had gone and James went back into the classroom with Miss Johnson.

# 3.GETTING HOME

James went home from school in the taxi and Mum was there, waiting at the door when he arrived. She asked if he'd had a good day at school and James grinned. Then Mum asked where his cakes were. Had he forgotten them? He must have done! Oh, no, he loved cakes and he liked to be able to give ones he'd made to Mum, Dad and Megan! Where could they be?

Then Mum looked at his home/school book and said that he didn't make cakes because Mrs Jones wasn't there. James remembered. It wasn't fair – that was what should have been happening today and he wanted chocolate cake. He threw his bag on the floor just as Mum read some more and reminded him he had to do some homework. He didn't want to do school work at home! Mum picked up his bag, saying that they

# How do you think James is feeling right now?

might as well do it straight away and got out the work which looked just like he had been given that morning – the type he couldn't do because it was different!

James shouted that he wasn't doing it. He didn't know what he had to do and he couldn't do it! He jumped out of his chair, knocking the drink that Mum had put out for him all over his school work. James ran up to his room, slammed the door behind him and leaped, face down on his bed. He hated school, he hated work, he hated ... James heard the door open quietly ... he hated everyone who came into ... Oh, it was Buddy. Buddy came and sat with him on the bed so James could put his arms right round him and rest his head against Buddy's soft fur. "I know," said James, "You're going to show me my colour chart. You don't need to. I remember." It didn't take long this time for James to get right down to green, with

# How do you think James is feeling right now?

Buddy's warm fur to stroke. James felt sorry now. He'd shouted at Mum and spoiled his school work.

James went downstairs and told Mum he was sorry. Mum said that she was sorry, too. She should have read the message in the home/school book before she asked him about the cakes and then she would have realised that he had a different teacher and new work. Then she could have talked to him about it first and asked him to do it later. Mum managed to dry out the work from school and then, later on, when James had watched some TV and had a drink, they did it together. It was easy!

Later, James snuggled up in bed and smiled to himself. Chocolate cakes tomorrow. As his eyes closed he caught sight of a familiar face by the door. "Goodnight, Buddy, sleep tight," whispered James.

**Paula Spibey**

**Beth Wicks**

**Dr Emily Talbot**

**Lisa Turan**

**Paloma Pedrera**

**Diya Kapur**

**Paula Spibey**
When my son was born in 2002 I decided to take a break from my career to make the most of motherhood, little did I know that he was to acquire a brain injury and refractory epilepsy at the age of 7 so that time has since become a precious memory. I am now working, endlessly it seems, searching out and co-ordinating medical, behavioural and educational support to ensure he lives a bright, happy and inclusive life.

**Beth Wicks** is an experienced teacher who has worked with schools and families as an independent education consultant specialising in the needs of young people with acquired brain injuries for many years. She is now semi-retired but delighted to be involved with projects such as this.

**Dr Emily Talbot** is a Clinical Psychologist who works within a Paediatric Neuropsychology Service in an acute NHS hospital trust in the UK. Emily works with children with acquired brain injury (ABI) and other neurological conditions. It was her work and contact with these young people that fuelled her collaboration with this book project to provide children, their families and teachers with a resource to support them in managing the emotional, behavioural and cognitive difficulties that can persist following brain injury in childhood.

**Lisa Turan** is the Chief Executive of the Child Brain Injury Trust . She has worked with the charity since 2003, specialising in developing services and information resources for families affected by childhood acquired brain injury.

**Paloma Pedrera** is a graduate in Fine Arts who has specialized in Illustration. Currently she is living in Loughborough, UK, working as a graphic designer for children's products. During her free time she likes to paint, draw and develop personal projects and her artistic skills.

**Diya Kapur** is a Graphic Design postgraduate from Nottingham Trent University, specialising in publication design. Currently she is working as a graphic designer in Mumbai, India. She loves designing books for children, and enjoys creating visual communication.